To all the children of the world, in the hope that the
Kite of Dreams helps them discover true happiness.

— Pilar López Ávila, Paula Merlán & Concha Pasamar —

This book is printed on **Stone Paper** with silver **Cradle to Cradle™** certification.

Cradle to Cradle™ is one of the most demanding ecological certification systems, awarded to products that have been conceived and designed in an ecologically intelligent way.

Cradle to Cradle™ recognizes that environmentally safe materials are used in the manufacturing of Stone Paper which have been designed for re-use after recycling. The use of less energy in a more efficient way, together with the fact that no water, trees nor bleach are required, were decisive factors in awarding this valuable certification.

The authors and the illustrator donate half of their income from this work to the Agua de Coco Foundation (www.aguadecoco.org).

The Kite of Dreams
Text © 2019 Pilar López Ávila and Paula Merlán
Illustrations © 2019 Concha Pasamar
This edition © 2019 Cuento de Luz SL
Calle Claveles, 10 | Urb. Monteclaro | Pozuelo de Alarcón | 28223 | Madrid | Spain
www.cuentodeluz.com
Original title in Spanish: *La cometa de los sueños*
English translation by Jon Brokenbrow
Printed in PRC by Shanghai Chenxi Printing Co., Ltd. August 2019, print number 1695-11
ISBN: 978-84-16733-68-2

The Kite
of Dreams

Pilar López Ávila
Paula Merlán
Concha Pasamar

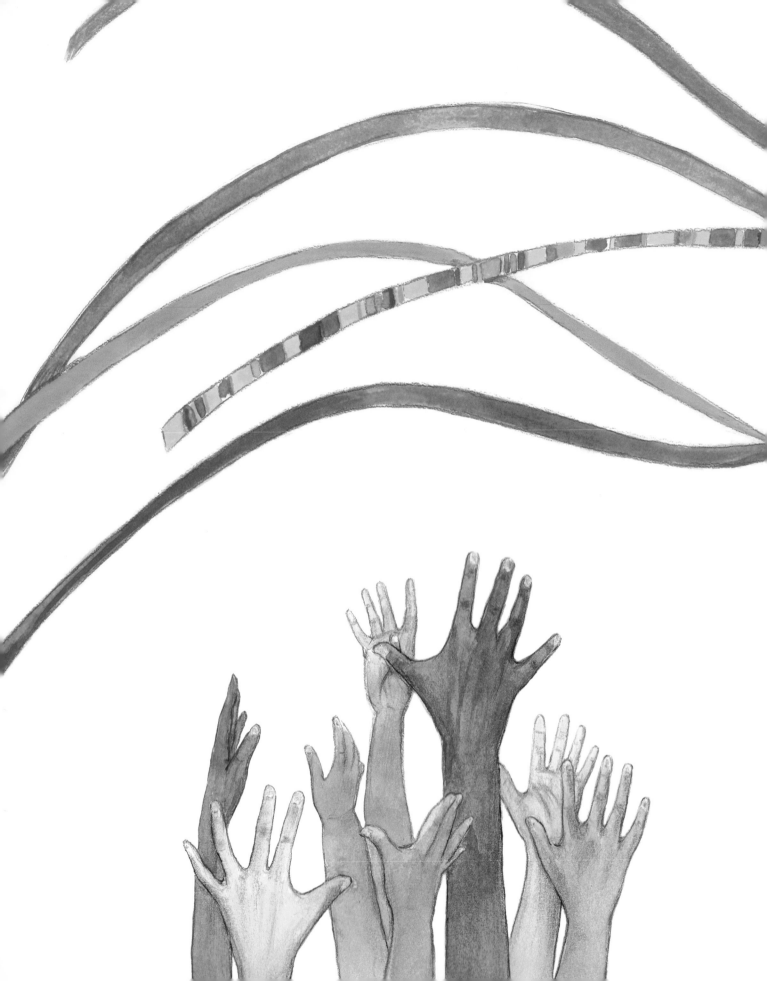

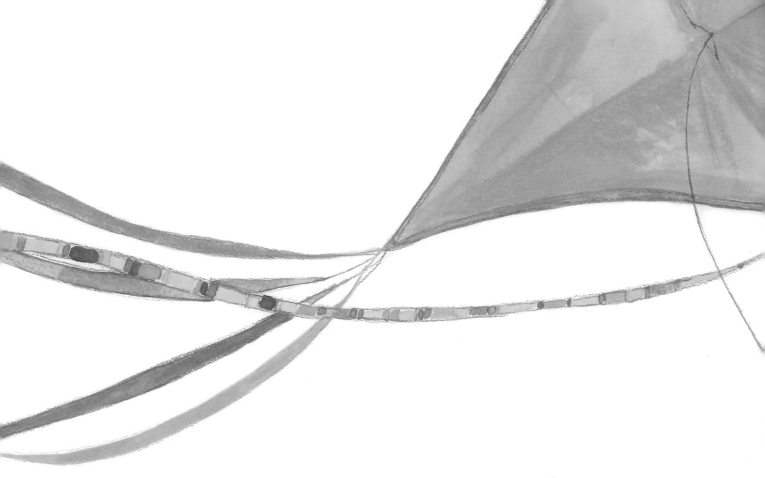

The Kite of Dreams sails through the air,
gathering the hopes and dreams of children around the world.

If you want to come along, hold onto its tail tightly.

Let yourself fly above the clouds, with nothing but the sound
of the wind in your face.

Fill your heart with happiness.
And dream of a better world.

On the Portuguese coast, looking out towards the vast Atlantic Ocean, Amalia listens to the music of the waves in the shells and scans the horizon for the whales and dolphins that accompany the Queen of the Seas.

She plays with her white kite, and dreams of an ocean that is clean, without plastic that wraps around the necks of the sea birds.

She imagines it without tin cans that glitter like fish scales, tricking seals into swallowing them.

And she hopes for an ocean with no discarded nets that trap sea turtles.

Amalia knows that the shimmering lights in the waves are stars that have fallen from the sky.

Juana lives in the south of Bolivia. She's ten years old, but she already has to work to help out her family. All she has to eat is a little piece of bread before she sets out to work. Every time she uses her cloth, she dreams.

Juana's kite is yellow, like the sun. It flies so high, it reaches the stars. She can almost touch them. Juana looks down on the world from high above and feels like nothing bad can happen to her. She reaches the moon, where she reads her favorite stories.

Suddenly, the noise of the city brings her back to reality.

Juana looks back up into the sky, with hope in her heart.

Mohesiwä dips his blowpipe darts in curare.
The poison paralyzes the animals he hunts.
He learned to do it from his tribe, the Yanomami,
who live in the Amazon rainforest.

Mohesiwä sees a strange bird flying between the trees in the forest and runs after it through the early morning mist.

Mohesiwä has never seen a kite before.

He makes a wish: to always live in his little patch of jungle, only taking what he needs, far away from the machines that chop down the trees, and the people who shout threats.

He wants to continue watching the parrots as they fly, happy and free. And to decorate his body with their feathers.

A hummingbird flies over a hilltop in Haiti.

It is the kite of Eliasen's dreams.

Eliasen is barefoot and she washes her feet in puddles.
She helps her mother sell coconut water and bananas to
the people traveling along the paths.

When the wind starts to blow, announcing the arrival of
the afternoon rains, Eliasen climbs to the very top of the hill,
to fly her hummingbird kite.

Then she runs back to her wooden hut and dreams of a home
made of concrete blocks that cannot be blown away by
the hurricanes.

It starts to rain.

Mexico is flooded. It has rained too much.

Lis wanders down the road, heading nowhere in particular, until she finds a piece of cloth. It is torn, but has a beautiful pattern. She has always loved sewing and she fixes it. She looks at it for a few seconds, then closes her eyes. The pattern makes her daydream of flowers, butterflies, and forests.

Lis makes the cloth into a kite and flies it with her brother.
They play, without being bothered by the shadow of violence.

When Lis dreams, she doesn't feel frightened any more,
and she wishes her life would be this way forever.

In San Diego, California, Matthew is waiting for his dad to come and pick him up.

They are going to go the beach to fly his kite, the one his dad gave him for his birthday, and which he hasn't tried out yet. Matthew has everything a boy could ever need to play and be happy.

But his dad is late, like he always is.

Then he gets a message on his phone.

Matthew walks back into the house, climbs the stairs to his room and puts the kite away again.

Maybe they can go tomorrow, or the next day . . .

On Cable Beach, in Australia, the sun is shining. Jack is running along the beach. He has forgotten his phone at home. That means he can look at everything around him. Some camels are running across the wet sand. Camels, in Australia! Jack wants to go and check them out.

But then he wonders if he has any messages, or any missed calls. A ragged cloth suddenly lands at his feet. He has an idea. His fingers move quickly, as if by magic. With just a few sticks and some string, he's made his own kite.

When he flies it, Jack daydreams about his mom. He misses her so much! She works too hard and she's so far away.

Jack thinks about her and keeps on flying his kite as the sun slowly sets.

Tonight wasn't a good night for Edwin.

He was sleeping rough with some other boys and girls, when they were woken up by angry voices, and they had to run away. They hide under a highway bridge, which is safer, but more uncomfortable.

As the sun rises, Edwin goes to the homeless children's center in Manila, in the Philippines. They give him something to eat and he goes to class to learn to read and write.

In the afternoon, Edwin heads back onto the streets, where he feels freer.

Free like the kite he will buy someday.

Although right now, all he can think about is survival, so the kite will have to wait.

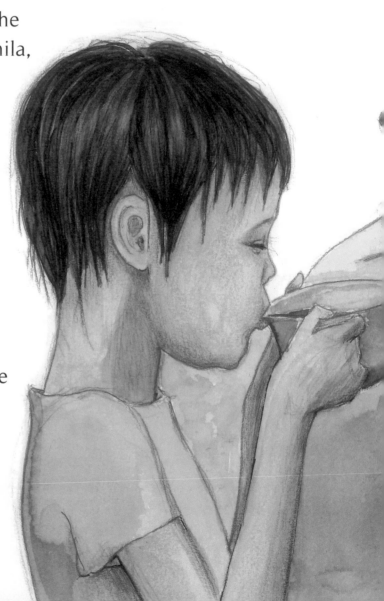

Xia lives in a village in China. She leaves home very early to go to school.

On the way, she meets up with her friends. But soon, Xia's happy expression changes and she begins to tremble.

To reach her school, she has to climb a steep, dangerous cliff.

She feels frightened for a moment. But Xia knows a trick that always works. She holds on tightly to the wooden ladder. She pretends a kite is carrying her up into the air, and she thinks about the experiment they did in class the day before, about the numbers game they will play in math class, and the play she has to learn for her theater class. Xia dreams of becoming a teacher one day.

Finally she reaches the top of the cliff and continues on her way. She's done it another day.

Chandra had to leave school when she was only twelve years old, because her parents needed her to help chop firewood, fetch water, or go to the marketplace to buy rice.

She is the youngest of six children, and lives in Nepal, in the mountains of Bhojpur.

Her name means 'moon.'

Chandra likes to run. She dreams of being a great athlete one day, running faster than the wind that blows the other children's kites into the air, and knows that one day she will take part in an important race.

Until then, Chandra runs and races against the wind that blows her kite of dreams into the air.

Vanko lives in the Ukraine. Many years ago, the radiation that escaped from Chernobyl changed his family forever.

The food he eats, and even the air he breathes, are bad for his health.

He wishes he could move far, far away, breathe clean air, fly over the mountains, swim in the rivers, and walk without being afraid of anything . . .

His kite lets him fly with his imagination all the way to Spain. Every year, he spends his summers there with other children his age. Vanko dreams of all the fun he will have when he gets there.

Amunet wants to be an archaeologist. She'd love to find hidden treasures, long-forgotten pharaohs, and buried mummies.

Amunet is very brave, and she wants to go to university in Cairo, but it won't be easy. Her mom has always told her so.

Suddenly, the image of a kite in the shape of a pyramid pops into her head. The wind blows it into her hands and she plays with it. Amunet whispers her most precious dream to the wind. And immediately, she feels something quite extraordinary.

Anja wakes up very early and shakes Tovo. If they arrive before the others, they may just find something valuable.

But even though they've woken up early, there are already lots of people searching amongst the trash in the biggest dump in Antananarivo, in Madagascar.

Tovo is little, but he's smart, and that's why he often finds things everyone else has missed: plastic bottle tops, copper wire, or screws. Anja feels happy to have her brother with her and hopes he will always be at her side.

Tovo finds a broken kite with colored ribbons. Together they fix it using a garbage bag. This afternoon they will fly it in the wind that blows over the dump, where their young hearts beat strongly.

From his neighborhood in the country of Angola, Adilson looks down to the beach. He is unhappy, because his kite fell into the sea, and now it is too wet and dirty to fly.

Some women are catching fish along the shore, while Adilson digs a hole that soon fills with a black, sticky liquid. His dad says that if the oil belonged to everyone, they would never be poor and hungry again.

With luck, Adilson will get a few coins for filling gallon bottle with oil so he can buy something to eat and then he will sit on the sand.

He dreams of watching the sun set over a sea that one day will be so clean, it will never get his kite dirty again.

Ángel is playing in the sunflower fields on the coast of Valdoviño, in Spain. The wind makes his kite soar high, high into the sky. Ángel tries to hold on tight, but it flies away. He is not worried though.

He smiles because the air is full of kites from around the world!

Their dreams have all come together and made them stronger. The tails of the kites hold on tightly to hope. Their rods are held in place by love. And their colors are those of absolute joy.